Totally AMAZING

NATURAL DISASTERS

 A GOLDEN BOOK • NEW YORK

Golden Books Publishing Company, Inc., New York, New York 10106

Nature's

Natural disasters are massive catastrophes that strike the world from time to time. Disasters can be caused by ferocious weather, or by powerful movements inside the Earth. Some even come from space!

Wild

A Big, Fiery Cauldron

Earth is covered with plates of solid rock which float on a sea of scorching hot melted rock, called magma. Most of the time the plates float peacefully, but...

Hot Shots

...when the plates move apart or slide under each other, the fiery magma bubbles up between the plates and explodes onto the surface of the Earth.

Cracking Up

When the plates grind against each other with a shudder, the ground shakes and buildings crumble. An earthquake has begun!

Disasters Are Deadly

Natural disasters are awesome t see but don't forget that often th kill many people. Experts try to g warnings before disasters happe But sometimes there's no time t escape. Then teams of rescuers rush to the scene to provide foo shelter, and medical help.

This tangled wreckage was once a row of houses. During a massive storm, fierce winds blew the buildings apart.

Exploding Volcanoes

Volcanoes are packed full of liquid rock called lava. Some volcanoes spurt out fountains of lava every day. Others sleep for thousands of years, then wake with a huge explosion. This supercharged bang can rip the volcano apart!

Return of the Ice Age

In the 1500s, two massive volcanoes erupted. They shot enormous clouds of ash into the sky, which blocked out the Sun. Europe turned icy cold and the Arctic Ocean froze over. Polar bears could have trekked across the frozen sea to visit new lands!

THE SLEEPING GIANT WAKES

1. Mount St. Helens volcano in Washington State lay asleep for 123 years. Then, in 1980, its sides began to bulge slowly outward.

2. Suddenly the volcano blew its top. Scorching ash and clouds of gas flew into the air. Nearby streams became so hot that fish leapt out of the water!

3. Snow on the sides of the volcano melted in seconds and mixed with the ash, creating monster mud flows that destroyed more than 200 homes.

4. Luckily, scientists had warned people living near the volcano that the blast was about to happen. Thousands were able to flee to safety.

...and Rivers of Fire!

Strange but True
Some types of lava travel slower than you walk. Others speed along at up to 31 miles (50 km) per hour.

HA HA! What do you call a volcano? A mountain with a hiccup! HEE HEE!

A fiery river of lava oozes down the slopes of this volcano in Hawaii, burning up everything in its path. When the lava cools, it blankets the land in solid, gray rock.

Cast in Stone

After a volcano erupts, things are never quite the same. The hot lava and ash cool and turn into hard rocks. Many of these rocks have weird shapes. Others hide incredible secrets.

Homes in Cones

These fairy-tale cones were left by volcanoes that erupted eight million years ago in Turkey. Rain washed away the softer parts of the cones to form caves where people made their homes. Today a few people still live here.

Smothered in Ash

In A.D. 79, in Italy, a giant volcano called Mount Vesuvius erupted. It showered the Roman town of Pompeii with scorching ash. People tried to flee but they were all buried alive. Eventually the ash turned to rock, trapp the unlucky victims forever in their stone tom

DISCOVERING THE PEOPLE OF POMPEII

1 Centuries later, archaeologists dug into the rock at Pompeii and discovered holes in the shape of people. The bodies in the holes had rotted away a long time ago.

2 The archaeologists used the holes as molds. They poured in runny plaster of Paris and waited for it to set.

3 When the plaster was dry, the archaeologists chipped away the surrounding rock. They were left with plaster models of the fleeing Romans and their pets!

This photograph of plaster-cast people from Pompeii shows how the force of the blast knocked everyone to the ground. It captures a gruesome scene frozen in time.

On the CRACK! Move

That's Weird

In 1995, an earthquake devastated Kobe, Japan, but the airport survived without a scratch. It rested on massive spongy feet that acted like giant cushions. The airport simply rode out the shakes.

When Earth's plates rub each other the wrong way, the ground jumps and rattles, causing an earthquake. Most earthquakes are so small that people don't notice them. But a major earthquake can destroy cities and even move mountains!

Making Waves

Earthquakes under the sea create the biggest waves in the world, called tsunamis. When a tsunami hits the coast, the massive wave can travel twice as fast as a racing car and may be three times higher than a house. It swallows everything in its path and then sucks it back out to sea.

The Great San Francisco Fire

In 1906, an earthquake hit San Francisco, causing a double disaster. First buildings toppled over. Then broken gas pipes, electricity wires, and stoves sparked off fires that burned down most of the city.

To the Rescue

After an earthquake, the race is on to find people trapped in the rubble. Specially trained dogs with supersensitive noses sniff their way toward a survivor. Then they bark the good news to a rescue team that pulls the person to safety.

A major earthquake is over in a few seconds but it can reduce a town to rubble.

Wild Winds

Hurricanes are fierce storms that set off the world's wildest winds. Over the sea, hurricane winds can whip up monster waves that sink ships. On land, they can rip up trees and blow down houses.

▲ In 1992 a mighty hurricane named Andrew battered the coast of Florida. Winds raced along at 175 miles (280 km) per hour, flinging boats onto the streets!

All in a Spin

This photograph, taken from space, shows a hurricane spinning across the ocean toward the United States. The most dangerous winds and the heaviest rains lurk in the thick white part of the storm.

Sneaky Storm

The center of a hurricane, called the eye, is completely still. When the eye passes over, everything is calm. You think the storm's finished, but really you're right in the middle of it. Spooky!

What's in a Name?

Every hurricane has a name to make it easy to identify. The first person to label hurricanes was a weather forecaster who lived in the 1800s. He named them after people he didn't like!

Where are my pail and shovel?

In Egypt strong winds fly across the desert and whip up wicked sandstorms called haboobs. The winds can smother whole villages, and even the ancient pyramids, in clouds of sand and dust.

Millions of years ago, scary sandstorms raged through the Gobi Desert in Asia, burying dinosaurs and their eggs. The hot sand kept the eggs perfectly preserved. So now, it's a top spot for dino-experts!

Terrible Twister

A tornado, or twister, is a deadly tube of wind that snakes down from the sky. When it hits the ground, it sucks up everything in its path like a monster-sized vacuum cleaner. A really powerful twister can even toss train cars into the air.

Are They Crazy?

When most people see a twister, they run quickly in the opposite direction. But storm chasers don't. They spend their time chasing twisters. Filming a pair of twisters, called sisters, would really make their day!

Touchdown

This deadly twister formed from storm clouds in Monument Valley in Arizona. When a twister hits the ground, it makes a deafening roar and dust shoots everywhere. It then spins along on a journey of destruction.

Lucky Escape

In 1986, in China, a tornado picked up 13 school children and carried them through the air for 12 miles (19 km). When it put them down again, they were completely unharmed!

**Strange
but True**

A waterspout may suck up fish as it moves across the water. When the spout stops spinning, the fish rain down on people's heads.

When a tornado forms over seas or lakes, it whips up the surface of the water into a tall, spinning column, called a waterspout.

Flood Alert

Rain is the all-time biggest cause of natural disasters. Short downpours flood houses in a flash and nonstop rain leads to even bigger trouble. Rivers swell until they burst, gushing out gallons of muddy water for miles.

THE GREAT FLOOD

The Bible tells how, long ago, God decided to send a mighty flood to punish all the bad people in the world. He told a man named Noah to build a boat called an ark. God wanted to save Noah's family and two of every kind of animal.

The rain fell for 40 days and 40 nights. The flood rose so high, it covered the highest mountains. But Noah's ark floated safely.

At last the waters dropped and the ark landed on a mountaintop. Noah and the animals began a new life, and God promised never to send another great flood.

That's Weird

Floods even happen in deserts. When a storm breaks out in nearby hills, water races down the slopes. Then, it surges along channels in the dry desert, sweeping up everything in its path.

Flying Cows

Often, the only way for people to escape a major flood is by helicopter—and animals are not forgotten, either! A helicopter picks up stranded cows and sheep. The confused creatures are put in a harness and carried up, up, and away.

High and Dry

In some hot countries many people live high up off the ground in houses on stilts. These people know that every year during the rainy season, rain pours nonstop for days on end. While towns and villages flood, these smart people stay safe and dry in their high-rise homes.

These men are fishing in the road during a flood. They could be here a long time—flood water can take weeks to drain away completely.

White Out

Wicked winter weather brings extra-special dangers. Wild snowstorms trap people in their homes. Scarier still, mighty avalanches charge down mountain slopes. These giant snowslides sweep up everything in their way.

Believe It or Not

Each year, about 100,000 avalanches plunge down the Rocky Mountains. Luckily, people are rarely hurt.

Monster Drifts

Blizzards are a deadly duo of heavy snowfall and strong winds. The bone-chilling blasts quickly drive snow into massive piles called drifts. The most dastardly drifts grow three or four times higher than an adult. That's tall enough to bury a house.

Avalanche on Its Way!

A snowstorm is a recipe for an avalanche. When snow on a mountainside grows too heavy, it suddenly falls away. As the icy load tumbles, it picks up speed—and more snow—until millions of tons of snow roar along. In a race with a car whizzing by at 60 miles (100 km) per hour, an avalanche would win.

"Now, where's my house?"

It's almost impossible to walk or even to see in a blizzard. Fierce winds blast snow around until everything is a white blur.

Tell Me Why

PEOPLE SHOOT AT SNOW

During World War I, avalanches were used as weapons. Soldiers fighting in mountains in France fired guns at snowy ledges above their enemy's camp. The shots triggered avalanches that buried the enemy soldiers in snow.

Today experts fire special guns at snow above mountain villages to protect people who live there. The small explosions set off harmless mini-avalanches. This stops the snow from building up and setting off a huge, killer avalanche.

A Dry Spell

A drought is a long stretch of hot, dry weather that may go on for months or years. During a serious drought, streams dry up and green fields turn to dusty deserts.

Thirsty Work

Day after day of scorching heat bakes the earth so hard that it cracks. Cattle kick up dust as they stampede across the bone-dry ground looking for food and water. Often they trek for hundreds of miles before coming across a water hole.

A BIG BOWL OF DUST

In the 1930s, a drought hit the Midwest. It barely rained for 10 years! All the farmers' crops died because there was no water.

Then the ground became dry and dusty. Winds blew the dust into blinding clouds that blocked out the sun and choked the birds.

Millions of people abandoned their homes. They left a string of empty ghost towns that stretched all the way from Texas to Canada.

Beating the Heat

A few places are struck by droughts again and again. When this happens, it's best to go to the source of the problem. People take to the skies in special airplanes. Their mission? To fire chemicals at the clouds to force out reluctant raindrops.

Forest trees and bushes become hot and dry during a drought. The tiniest spark can set off a raging fire that may blaze for days.

Threats from Outer

Thousands of rocks called asteroids whiz through space. Most of the time, they circle the Sun, but now and again they head straight for us. Big collisions are rare, but when they happen, they're truly earth-shattering!

▲ Asteroids come in different shapes and sizes. They can be as small as a pebble or almost as large as a planet. Large asteroids can be hundreds of miles across.

Lucky Escape

In 1996 an asteroid missed Earth by only 280,000 miles (450,000 km). It came as close to us as the Moon. That might sound like a long distance but, in space terms, it's a bit too close for comfort!

Dino-disaster

Many scientists blame an enormous asteroid for wiping out the dinosaurs 65 million years ago. When the rock crashed, the explosion threw up a dust cloud that blocked out the Sun. Earth became so dark and cold that all the dinosaurs died out.

Space

Space Invader

About 22,000 years ago, a massive meteorite crash-landed in the Arizona desert. It created this huge crater. You could lay three Empire State Buildings across the crater, from end to end.

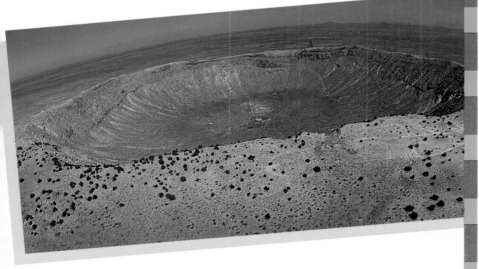

Every day, Earth is pummeled by tiny space rocks. Luckily for us, most of them burn up in the atmosphere and become shooting stars. On a clear night, you can see these "stars" as streaks of light shooting across the sky.

The Moon has no atmosphere to protect it from falling space rocks, so it gets a real hammering. Its surface is dotted with as many as three billion craters!

Disaster

Scientists

Check out these disaster scientists and their amazing disaster-detecting gadgets. These guys are just looking for trouble! They can't stop storms or earthquakes, but they can try to warn people in time.

THE WEATHER WATCHERS
Meteorologists work in weather centers, where they gather all kinds of information about dangerous weather. They watch how weather changes and where it's heading.

Satellites high above Earth beam back pictures of clouds.

Crews on ships and in airplanes send in weather reports from faraway places.

Volcano Doctors

Vulcanologists are a bit like doctors. They have the hot job of studying volcanoes. First they check a volcano's sides to see if they are bulging with hot magma. Then, the hot docs prod the volcano with a gas detector, looking for telltale signs of escaping gases.

WEATHER CENTER

Radar picks up signs of rain.

Inside the weather center, superfast computers make sense of all this information.

Creepy Shakes

It's difficult to tell when an earthquake will happen or how big it will be. A clever machine, called a creepmeter, helps scientists predict earthquakes. It picks up tiny shivers in the ground which could mean that something much bigger is on the way.

That's Weird

Often animals give the first warning of an earthquake. Worms, snakes, rats, and mice have been known to scramble out of their holes just before the rumbles start.

These scientists are launching a giant weather balloon. Its onboard gadgets will measure what's happening in the clouds.

Fantastic Tales

Long ago, people blamed nature's terrifying powers on monsters or angry gods and told incredible stories about their dastardly deeds. Natural events are no longer a mystery, but they make for action-packed movies!

That's Weird

Long ago, in Mexico, the Aztecs believed that a god lived inside the violent volcano above their city. Often they threw young girls into the volcano, hoping that their gruesome gifts would stop the god from blowing the volcano's top.

FISH IN A FLAP

In ancient Japan, people believed that earthquakes were caused by a giant catfish that lived underground. When it wriggled in the mud, the ground shook so much that a quake began.

The gods tried to keep the flapping fish out of trouble. They pinned it down under a heavy rock so that it couldn't move.

Then, one day, a massive quake destroyed the ancient city of Edo. People believed that the catfish had wriggled free while the gods were away.

Mischievous Mouse

The Native American Chippewa people of Ohio have a tale to explain floods—they blame them on a mouse! In their story, the Sun's heat is stored in a bag. The pesky mouse nibbles a hole in the corner of the bag and the heat leaks out. The escaping warmth melts all the mountain snow, which floods the land.

24

The Lost World

The ancient Greeks thought that their god Zeus started earthquakes when he lost his temper. One story tells how Zeus flew into a rage with the people of a magical island called Atlantis. He sent a quake that sank their island without a trace. Today a few people still wonder if this land ever really existed.

An Event...

When in Southern California visit UNIVERSAL STUDIOS TOUR

TON HESTON
ARDNER • GEORGE KENNEDY
GREENE • GENEVIEVE BUJOLD • RICHARD ROUNDTREE
MARJOE GORTNER • BARRY SULLIVAN • LLOYD NOLAN • VICTORIA PRINCIPAL
GEORGE FOX and MARIO PUZO Music by JOHN WILLIAMS Produced and Directed by MARK ROBSON
oducer JENNINGS LANG • A MARK ROBSON-FILMAKERS GROUP PRODUCTION
ORIGINAL SOUNDTRACK AVAILABLE ON MCA RECORDS & TAPES
A UNIVERSAL PICTURE • TECHNICOLOR® PANAVISION®
PG PARENTAL GUIDANCE SUGGESTED

Earthquake shows Los Angeles in the grip of a huge quake. When the movie first played, a clever device in theaters shook the audience in their seats so they felt like they were part of the action!

HA HA! What do people drink during an earthquake? Milkshakes! HEE HEE!

There may be Trouble

It's a fact—the world is overheating. Every day humans blast out hot polluting fumes into the delicate atmosphere above Earth. No one really knows what will happen next or if new kinds of natural disasters lie ahead.

Believe It or Not

A few scientists think that Earth is heating up naturally. The fumes that we release into the air just make it happen more quickly.

That's Weird

When cows burp, they give off huge amounts of a world-warming gas called methane!

Turning up the Heat

Earth is kept cozy and warm by a special layer of gases in the atmosphere that traps some of the Sun's heat. Without this layer, Earth would be deathly cold. But cars and factories pump out heat-trapping gases such as carbon dioxide, which means that too much heat is being kept in!

There is too much carbon dioxide reaching the atmosphere.

When factories and cars burn fuel, they release carbon dioxide.

Ahead

Meltdown

A few scientists believe that in the future, the world could be so warm that the gigantic sheets of ice that cover the North and South Poles will melt. The melting ice will gush out huge amounts of water into the world's oceans. Low-lying shores will flood and islands in many parts of the world will disappear completely.

A Whole Load of Hurricanes

A heated-up world could also mean bigger and meaner storms than ever before! Baby storm clouds love to feed off the steamy air that rises from warm water. It gives them the strength to grow into monster hurricanes.

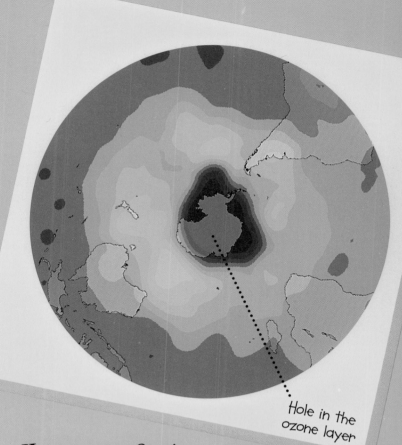

Hole in the ozone layer

Hole in the Sky!

High above Earth, there is a layer of invisible gas called ozone. It protects our skin from the Sun's harmful rays. But now scientists have spotted a hole in the ozone layer, and some of those deadly rays are getting through.

Frightful Fridges

Some of the villains causing the ozone hole are spray cans and refrigerators. Often these household objects contain chemicals called chlorofluorocarbons, or CFCs. These nasty chemicals escape into the atmosphere and gobble up the ozone that floats there.

Hot Spots

Several places are in the hot seat when it comes to natural disasters. These hot spots are more likely to be hit than anywhere else in the world. Here's a guide to the danger zones.

Ring of Fire

United States of America

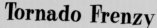

Tornado Frenzy
Each year, about 1,000 tornadoes spin across the United States. Most happen in the Midwest.

Earthquake Zone
The San Andreas Fault is a long stretch of shaky ground along the coast of California. Here, big cities are in the firing line for earthquakes.

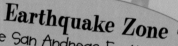

Not a Drop
The Sahel in Africa is the world's worst area for droughts. For up to three years, this hot dusty region may have no rain, while rain pours down on lands nearby.

Pacific Ocean

Ring of Fire

Key

tornadoes

droughts

volcanoes

floods

earthquakes

hurricanes

icy winds

Ring of Fire

The edge of the Pacific Ocean is an explosive place. Three quarters of the world's active volcanoes lie here in a circle called the Ring of Fire.

Raining Again

For up to half a year, the northwest of India may be flooded by rainstorms brought by monsoon winds. For the rest of the year, hardly any rain falls!

Pacific Ocean

Philippine Islands

India

Africa

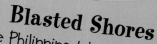

Blasted Shores

The Philippine Islands are the top hurricane hot spot. Each summer, the islands are pounded by hurricanes. When one leaves, often another one arrives.

Ice King

The land around the South Pole, called Antarctica, suffers the worst winter storms. Icy snow blasts along as fast as a speeding car.

Antarctica

Nature's Most Wanted

Natural disasters are the world's worst troublemakers. They break all the rules and cause havoc wherever they go. Here are some of the worst offenders.

Angry Andrew

Hurricane Andrew was the most expensive natural disaster ever in the United States. One morning, in 1992, its billowing winds tore through Florida, toppling homes and battering yachts. It caused $30 billion worth of damage. That's more money than all the state lottery jackpots combined!

Twister Gangs

America is never safe from the threat of twisters. In one single month in 1995, a gang of nearly 400 tornadoes terrorized 36 states. Eighty-six of the twisters appeared on one single day.

Terrible Trio

In May 1970, the town of Yungay in Peru was hit three times in a row. First its residen were shaken out of bed by an earthquake. Next the town flooded and finally it was engulfed by a monster mudslide.

Undercover Agents

Not all volcanoes are bad guys! Many volcanoes are wanted for their hot properties. Volcanic rocks heat up water underground. In Iceland, this hot water is piped into people's homes, straight into their bathrooms.

Smoke Screen

Volcanoes cause record-breaking explosions. They can blow an incredible 1.8 million cubic feet (50,000 cubic meters) of hot ash and rocks into the air. That's enough to fill the Great Pyramid in Egypt 50 times over!

Index and Glossary

Illustrations: Gary Bines, Gary Boller
Consultants: Dr. Brian Baptie (geologist), Rodney Blackall (meteorologist)
Authors: Sarah Fecher, Clare Oliver
Photographs: Cover: Tony Stone Images; p1:Tony Stone Images; p3: Pictor; p7: Planet Earth Pictures; p8: Powerstock/Zefa; p9: Colorific!; p11: Science Photo Library; p12: Oxford Scientific Films; p13: Planet Earth Pictures; p14: Tony Stone Images; p15: Planet Earth Pictures, p17: Colorific!; p18/19: Tony Stone Images; p20: Powerstock/Zefa; p21: Craig Fujii/Seattle Times; p23: Science Photo Library; p24: Science Photo Library; p25: Science Photo Library; p27: Universal, courtesy of the Kobal Collection; p29: Science Photo Library; p30: Image Bank; p31: FLPA.